Howard B. Wigglebottom

Blends in Like Chameleons:
A Fable About Belonging

Howard Binkow
Susan F. Cornelison

Howard Binkow
Rev. Ana Rowe
Illustrated by Susan F. Cornelison
Book design and front cover by Jane Darroch Riley

Thunderbolt Publishing
We Do Listen Foundation
www.wedolisten.com

This book is the result of a joint creative effort with Rev. Ana Rowe and Susan F. Cornelison.

Gratitude and appreciation are given to all those who reviewed the story prior to publication.
The book became much better by incorporating several of their suggestions:

Joanne De Graaf, Kay Marner and teachers, librarians, counselors and students at:

Bossier Parish Schools, Bossier City, Louisiana
Central Elementary, Beaver Falls, Pennslyvania
Chalker Elementary, Kennesaw, Georgia
Charleston Elementary, Charleston, Arkansas
Forest Avenue Elementary, Hudson, Massachusetts
Garden Elementary, Venice, Florida
Glen Alpine Elementary, Morganton, North Carolina
Golden West Elementary, Manteca, California
Hartsdale Avenue Public School, Mississauga, Ontario, Canada
Indian Neck School, Branford, Connecticut

Iveland Elementary School, St. Louis, Missouri
Kincaid Elementary, Marietta, Georgia
Lamarque Elementary School, North Port, Florida
Lee Elementary, Los Alamitos, California
Prestonwood Elementary, Dallas, Texas
Sherman Oaks Elementary, Sherman Oaks, California
Sollars Elementary School, Misawa Air Force Base, Japan
Walt Disney Magnet School, Chicago, Illinois
West Navarre Primary, Navarre, Florida

Printed in Singapore by Tien Wah Press (Pte) Limited.
First printing May 2011
ISBN 978-0-9826165-5-0
LCCN 2011925896

Last fall when Joey, the new kid on the block, walked into Howard's class, everything changed …

… Joey didn't listen and he couldn't sit still. He didn't share, didn't wait for his turn or follow school rules. On top of it all, Joey felt there must be something wrong with him.

No one liked Joey. Everyone stayed away from him. Everyone, that is, but Howard, who felt sorry for him.

Howard would like things in school to go back to the way they were: calm and quiet. If he only knew how!

A month later, at lunch, Joey said: "Hey, Howard! Look what I brought in my lunch box today!" Howard looked in and saw two chameleons peeking out.

"I named them Camille and Leon-get it?"

Joey said loudly.

Howard knew this couldn't be good: It was definitely against the school rules.

Before Joey could close the lid, the little guys escaped and made a big commotion! Joey was sent to the principal. Howard had to find the chameleons and put them back in the box.

They were very hard to catch because chameleons are great at hide-and-seek. They also change colors and match whatever they land on.

After many tries, Howard gave up.

When Howard saw Joey after school, he asked,
"What are you going to do to stay out of trouble?"

"I don't know. I try really hard but I can't pay attention or behave like you all do. Nobody likes me, not even the teacher. There must be something wrong with me," answered Joey.

"I'm sorry you feel bad. I bet we can make it better. Oh wow! I just remembered the chameleons are still loose. Let's go. I'll help you catch them," said Howard.

Help find the chameleons.

They found Camille and Leon at the corner store making a big mess. The cashier yelled, "Put the chameleons back in the box and leave!!"
"See?" said Joey. "Everybody is always getting mad at me."

Howard was tired and sad by the time they got to Joey's place. How was he going to help his friend?

"Oops," said Joey, "they just escaped again! I'll be in trouble if I don't find them." They looked everywhere but there was just too much stuff and a gazillion places for two chameleons to hide.

Help find the chameleons.

18

Then Howard had an idea. "Let's do like the chameleons: They match whatever they land on. When you want to be on the same team as everyone else you do just like them. If everyone in class is paying attention and following rules, you match that. If no one brings pets, you match it. Get it?"

Help find the chameleons.

21

Moments later Joey's mother walked in.

"Snacks, anyone?" she offered. "Howard, how wonderful of you to help Joey clean up this mess. What a great friend you are!"

"Yes, he is!" said Joey. "Mom, I'm going to do like the chameleons! No one will be mad at me anymore and I will feel good!"

"What does that mean?" asked his mother.

Help find the chameleons.

23

"Nobody likes me," said Joey. "I get angry and do silly things when I can't follow the rules or pay attention–that happens to me a lot.

"If I play like the chameleons and do what the other kids are doing in the classroom, I'll stay out of trouble and will be part of their team."

"Oh, Joey," sighed his mom, "I'm so sorry you are going through this. First thing Monday we will go talk to your teacher."

So his mom went to school and met with the teacher and then the school counselor.

"Many kids have a hard time sitting still, paying attention and finishing tasks. They don't make friends and feel there is something wrong with them," said the counselor. "We have a plan that will help Joey."

PLAN FOR JOEY
Simple Social Rules
• • •

27

By springtime, with help from those around him, Joey was doing much better. He felt good about himself!

Howard was happy to help a friend and even happier things in school went back to normal, the same as before. Well, almost the same …

Howard B. Wigglebottom Blends in Like Chameleons
Suggestions for Lessons and Reflections

★ **THERE MUST BE SOMETHING WRONG WITH ME**

Joey felt there was something wrong with him. He couldn't sit still or pay attention. He couldn't follow or remember rules or instructions. He couldn't finish tasks.

Do you know anyone like Joey? Are you like Joey sometimes? There are many ways to learn new things: Some children learn by looking at pictures, others by listening to stories and songs, others by touching and building things. Some need to sit still, but kids like Joey like to be moving all the time—that is how they learn the best.

There is nothing wrong with Joey. If he can stand up and move while the other kids sit still, he will also be able to pay attention, remember the rules and finish his tasks.

Joey also felt nobody liked him. He wondered if getting angry and doing silly things had something to do with it. Did you like Joey? Why do you think nobody liked him? Why do you think he was angry? He was often angry because he couldn't learn like everyone else. Most of us do silly things when we are angry. What do you do when you are angry?

★ **SYMPATHY AND EMPATHY**

The children didn't understand or like Joey, except for Howard. Howard felt sorry for him. He could tell Joey was having a hard time. Making friends with Joey was a very nice thing to do. When Howard got to know Joey better he started to like him a lot: He was fun, nice and very smart.

Adults have a saying: "Don't judge the book by its cover." Can you tell if a book is good or bad just by the cover? When you first meet a new kid and you don't like what you see, give it a chance. Most of us don't like things that we're not used to, or people who look and behave very differently from us. After some time, we get used to the differences and start to like them.

How come Howard brought a chameleon to class at the end of the story? Was it wrong? Yes, it was against the rules, but Howard brought a chameleon to class to help Joey feel good and to show Joey he was on the same team, that he understood and shared the same things.

★ **WHEN WE LONG TO BELONG**

Joey wanted to fit in, to be part of the team, to be liked. What does it mean to be part of a team? A team is a group of kids who want the same things. They protect and respect and are nice to each other because they are on the same team.

Joey wasn't nice when he was angry. He didn't respect the social rules. Here are few social rules:

- Only take people's things with their permission.
- Stop when people ask you to.
- Say "thank you" and "please."
- Wash hands before eating and after going to the bathroom.
- Look people in the eyes.
- Be quiet when other people ask you to.
- Cover your mouth when you cough.
- Don't interrupt people when they are speaking.

Joey learned that if he wanted to be liked he needed to follow the social rules. Can you think of more social rules? Do you always follow the social rules?

★ BLENDING IN

Chameleons change colors: They match whatever color they land on. It is hard to tell where they are because they blend in.

What does it mean to blend in? It means when things mix well and we can't tell them apart anymore. Is there a blender where you live? If we place fruits and water in a blender and turn it on, what happens?

Why do chameleons blend in? It is for protection–they are hard to see. What other things besides chameleons and fruit can blend in? How about people? People say they want to "blend in" when they want to be part of the team, feel good and be liked. But people are different from chameleons, fruit or paint: You can always tell people apart. We all have different wishes, thoughts, feelings and desires (read the lesson in *Howard B. Wigglebottom Listens to His Heart*).

Being part of a team or blending in doesn't mean doing or saying things we don't want to. It means we are nice to everyone and we follow the social rules. Are the social rules the same everywhere? Most of them are the same, but depending on the country, there can be extra rules that we need to know about.

★ PEACE AND CALM

The classroom was quiet before Joey arrived. Howard liked it when things were calm–no fights and no yelling. That's why he wanted things to go back to the way they were. He knew that a calm, clean and peaceful room was the healthiest place to be and learn new things. When Joey got help and his needs were taken care of, he was able to follow the rules and everyone was happy and peaceful again. So if there is one kid in school who breaks the peace and calm, we all have to understand and help, so things can be nice as soon as possible.

Visit wedolisten.com for more information on children with special needs-ADHD

Learn more about Howard's other adventures.

BOOKS

Howard B. Wigglebottom Learns to Listen

Howard B. Wigglebottom Listens to His Heart

Howard B. Wigglebottom Learns About Bullies

Howard B. Wigglebottom Learns About Mud and Rainbows

Howard B. Wigglebottom Learns It's OK to Back Away

Howard B. Wigglebottom and the Monkey on His Back: A Tale About Telling the Truth

Howard B. Wigglebottom Learns Too Much of a Good Thing Is Bad

Howard B. Wigglebottom and the Power of Giving: A Christmas Story

WEBSITE

Visit www.wedolisten.com

- Enjoy free animated books, games and songs.
- Print lessons and posters from the books.
- Email the author.